THE SLY OLD CAT

THE SLY OLD CAT

WRITTEN AND ILLUSTRATED BY
BEATRIX POTTER

FREDERICK WARNE
LONDON AND NEW YORK

Published by: Frederick Warne & Co Ltd., London
Frederick Warne & Co Inc., New York

LIBRARY OF CONGRESS
CATALOGUE CARD No. 73 - 163984

ISBN 0 7232 1420 4
Printed in Great Britain by
Lowe & Brydone (Printers) Ltd, Thetford, Norfolk
1225.273

Foreword

Beatrix Potter wrote *The Sly Old Cat* in 1906 and if everything had gone according to plan it would have appeared a year later as another title in the famous *Peter Rabbit* series. Beatrix Potter had written this story for her publisher's little daughter, Nellie Warne, and she had set it out in panoramic form with the pictures and text mounted on linen and folded concertina-wise into a wallet—the same format as the 1906 editions of *The Story of the Fierce Bad Rabbit* and *The Story of Miss Moppet*. But before work could be started on the production of this story, booksellers became reluctant to stock these panoramic books because of the difficulty of refolding them after customers' handling, so for the time being nothing further was done with *The Sly Old Cat*.

Then in 1916 *Fierce Bad Rabbit* and *Miss Moppet* appeared in conventional book form,

and again the possibility of adding *The Sly Old Cat* to the series was considered, but although Beatrix Potter thought the story 'really amusing' and had no objection to its being published she did not feel inclined to prepare a new set of drawings from the preliminary sketches in Nellie Warne's manuscript. So once more *The Sly Old Cat* was returned to Nellie Warne.

Now this attractive little story is being published as a book for the first time, with Beatrix Potter's original sketches which, although not specially prepared for reproduction, have the life and expression and all the charm and spontaneity so characteristic of her preliminary work.

LESLIE LINDER

THE SLY OLD CAT

This is a sly old Cat, who gave
a tea-party to a rat.

This is the rat in his best
clothes coming down the area
steps. They had their tea in
the kitchen.

"How do you do? Mr. Rat!
Will you sit on this chair?"
said the Cat.

"I will eat *my* bread and butter first," said the Cat, "and then *you* shall eat the crumbs that are left, Mr. Rat!"

"This is a very rude way of treating visitors!" said Mr. Rat to himself.

"Now I will pour out *my* tea,"
said the Cat, "and you shall
lick up the drops that are left
in the milk jug, Mr. Rat; and
then *I* will have some dessert!"
said the Cat.

"I believe she is going to eat *me* for dessert; I wish I'd never come!" said poor Mr. Rat.

She tipped up the milk jug—
that greedy old Cat! she
didn't want to leave one single
drop for the rat.

But the rat jumped on the
table and gave the jug a pat,
and it slipped down quite
tight over the head of the Cat!

Then the Cat banged about
the kitchen with its head fast
in the jug,

and the rat sat on the table
drinking tea out of a mug.

Then he put a muffin in a
paper bag and went away.

And he ate the whole muffin at one sitting; so that is the end of the Rat.

And the Cat broke the jug against the leg of the kitchen table; so that is the end of the Cat.

March 20th 06.